Unicorn Princesses
FLASH'S DASH

Unicorn Princesses

FLASH'S DASH

Emily Bliss

illustrated by Sydney Hanson

BLOOMSBURY

NEW YORK LONDON OXFORD NEW DELHI SYDNEY

First published in the United States of America in August 2017
by Bloomsbury Children's Books
www.bloomsbury.com

Bloomsbury is a registered trademark of Bloomsbury Publishing Plc

For information about permission to reproduce selections from this book, write to
Permissions, Bloomsbury Children's Books, 1385 Broadway, New York, NY 10018
Bloomsbury books may be purchased for business or promotional use.
For information on bulk purchases please contact Macmillan Corporate and
Premium Sales Department at specialmarkets@macmillan.com

Library of Congress Cataloging-in-Publication Data
Names: Bliss, Emily, author. | Hanson, Sydney, illustrator.
Title: Flash's dash / by Emily Bliss ; illustrated by Sydney Hanson.
Description: New York : Bloomsbury, 2017. | Series: Unicorn princesses ; 2
Summary: Cressida is thrilled to be the first human to participate in the annual
Thunder Dash, but angry boulders and an inept wizard-lizard threaten to
ruin the competition.
Identifiers: LCCN 2016036844 (print) | LCCN 2017016398 (e-book)
ISBN 978-1-68119-330-4 (paperback) • ISBN 978-1-68119-329-8 (hardcover)
ISBN 978-1-68119-331-1 (e-book)
Subjects: | CYAC: Contests—Fiction. | Unicorns—Fiction. |
Princesses—Fiction. | Magic—Fiction. | Fantasy. | BISAC: JUVENILE
FICTION/Animals/Mythical. | JUVENILE FICTION/Fantasy & Magic. |
JUVENILE FICTION/Royalty.
Classification: LCC PZ7.1.B633 Fl 2017 (print) | LCC PZ7.1.B633 (e-book) |
DDC [Fic]—dc23
LC record available at https://lccn.loc.gov/2016036844

Book design by Jessie Gang
Typeset by Westchester Publishing Services
Printed and bound in the U.S.A. by Berryville Graphics Inc., Berryville, Virginia
2 4 6 8 10 9 7 5 3 1 (paperback)
2 4 6 8 10 9 7 5 3 1 (hardcover)

All papers used by Bloomsbury Publishing, Inc., are natural, recyclable products
made from wood grown in well-managed forests. The manufacturing processes
conform to the environmental regulations of the country of origin.

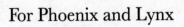
For Phoenix and Lynx

Unicorn Princesses

princesses

FLASH'S DASH

Chapter One

In the top tower of Spiral Palace, Ernest, a green wizard-lizard, placed two avocados on a chair. He smoothed his cape and straightened his pointy purple hat. With one scaly hand, he opened a thick, dusty book entitled *Intermediate Spells for Enterprising Wizard-Lizards.* With the other hand, he clutched a silver wand.

He cleared his throat. And then, reading from the book as he waved his wand at the avocados, he chanted, "Stickety Snickety Battery Goo! Pinkity Spinkity Strawberry Spew! Sleetily Sweetily Thickily Slew!" He waited. Nothing happened to the avocados. They didn't even quiver or jump.

"Huh," Ernest said. He repeated the spell. Again, nothing happened.

He wrinkled his brow and scratched his head. Then he checked his book. "Oh dear! Oh dear!" he muttered. "I read the wrong spell. Again. Oh dear! I thought that one sounded awfully strange."

Ernest rushed over to the window. Usually, when he cast the wrong spell, the sky darkened, thunder boomed, and lightning flashed. But this time the sun still shone in the cloudless blue sky above the Rainbow Realm. Just as he was about to breathe a sigh of relief, Ernest saw two bright pink clouds hovering over the Thunder Peaks. The clouds glittered and sparkled above the gold and silver mountains. And then, in a burst of light, the clouds vanished.

"Oh dear! I've done it again," Ernest muttered. "I guess I'll have to tell Flash." He sighed, scratched his head, and looked back at the avocados. He leafed through his book to find the spell he had meant to read, "Instructions for Turning Avocados into Flying Sneakers." And then, waving his wand, he chanted, "Fleetily Speedily

Fastily Foo! Wing Feet, Fleet Feet, Fast Feet, Blue!"

The two avocados trembled and spun in circles. They turned from purple to red to blue. And then, with a flash of gold so bright Ernest had to shield his eyes, two blue running shoes, each with a set of gold wings, appeared on the floor. Ernest

jumped with excitement and slid his scaly feet into the shoes.

"I did it! I did it!" he called out as he sprinted back and forth across the room. "Thunder Dash, here I come!"

Chapter Two

When Cressida Jenkins woke early on a Saturday morning, the unicorn lamp on her bedside table still glowed, and her book, *Valley of the Unicorns*, lay face down on her pillow. She had, once again, fallen asleep reading. Cressida glanced at her new rainbow clock. It was 6:56 a.m. She sat up. She yawned and stretched. And then she opened her bedside table drawer and pulled out the key the unicorn princesses had given to her. It was a large, old-fashioned silver key with a crystal ball handle that changed colors.

That morning, the key's handle glowed orange, like a jack-o'-lantern. Cressida wrapped her hands around the key and remembered how she'd gotten it. On a walk in the woods with her family, she had found the key under a giant oak tree and slipped it into her pocket. The next morning, worried someone—perhaps even a magical forest creature, like a fairy or a troll—might look for it, she returned to the woods to leave the key where she found it. That's when she met the key's owner, a yellow unicorn named Princess Sunbeam.

It turned out Sunbeam was searching for a human girl who believed in unicorns to help her find her magic gemstone—a yellow sapphire that had disappeared when Ernest the wizard-lizard accidentally cast the wrong spell.

Cressida accompanied Sunbeam to the Rainbow Realm, an enchanted world ruled by seven unicorn princesses who each wore a unique gemstone necklace that gave them magic powers. After Cressida found Sunbeam's yellow sapphire, the princesses gave Cressida her very own key to the Rainbow Realm. "You're welcome to visit anytime you want," Sunbeam had said. "And when we want to signal for you to return, we'll make the handle turn bright pink." Now

Cressida smiled, remembering that magic day with Sunbeam.

Since it was Saturday, and since she had already finished all her math and reading homework, Cressida decided to visit the Rainbow Realm that day. She missed her unicorn friends. But first she wanted to eat breakfast and read another chapter of her book. She only had four chapters left, and when she finished it she would have read every book about unicorns in her elementary school's library.

Cressida returned the key to her bedside table drawer and climbed out of bed. She peeled off her green unicorn pajamas, and put on rainbow leggings and a blue sweater with a purple sequined unicorn on the front. She tiptoed into the kitchen. Her older brother, Corey, and her parents were still asleep, and she didn't want to wake them. She poured herself a bowl of Whole Wheat Squares and ate her cereal quickly: she couldn't wait to get back to her book.

When she finished, Cressida put her empty bowl in the sink and crept back to her bedroom, climbed onto the bed, and found her place in *Valley of the Unicorns*. But after she had only read a few sentences, she heard a soft, high noise. It sounded, Cressida thought, like wind chimes or someone playing a triangle.

Cressida looked up. The noise went away. She waited several seconds, shrugged, and returned to her book. But just as she was about to turn to the next page, the chiming returned. Cressida listened for a moment. It sounded like it was coming from her bedside table drawer. She put down her book, opened the drawer, and pulled out the key again. The handle glowed bright pink and pulsed. She held the key up to her ear, and, sure enough, it was making the tinkling noise. Cressida grinned with excitement. The unicorn princesses were inviting her back to the Rainbow Realm!

Cressida bounded to her closet and slid her feet into her silver unicorn sneakers, which had bright pink lights that blinked every time she walked, ran, or jumped. She raced into the kitchen and left a note on the table for her parents saying she'd gone

for a quick walk. Luckily, when Cressida entered the Rainbow Realm, time in the human world froze. That meant she could stay with the unicorns as long as she wanted without her parents worrying about her or wondering where she was.

Gripping the key in her right hand, Cressida sprinted out her back door, bounded into the woods, and ran along the path that led to the oak tree. The pink lights on her sneakers blinked the whole way, and Cressida couldn't remember ever feeling so excited. Once she got to the oak tree, she kneeled down to the base of the trunk, near the roots. "Here I come!" Cressida whispered, and she pushed the key into the tiny keyhole Sunbeam had shown her.

With a jolt, the forest and sky began to spin, faster and faster, until all Cressida could see was a blur of brown, green, and blue. Then everything went pitch black, and she felt as though she were falling fast through space.

Suddenly, she landed on something soft and velvety. For a moment, she felt dizzy, and all she could see was a revolving blur of white, purple, pink, and silver. Soon, as Cressida blinked and took deep breaths, the room stopped spinning, and she knew exactly where she was: sitting on a plush purple armchair in Spiral Palace, the unicorn princesses' white, shimmering castle that was shaped like a giant unicorn horn.

Chapter Three

Cressida inhaled. The palace smelled like lavender, mint, and honey. Sunlight poured in through the floor-to-ceiling windows, and the purple velvet curtains swayed in the breeze. Cressida stood up. "Hello?" she called out. "It's me, Cressida!" She listened for the tapping of hooves against the marble floors, but all she heard was the faint sound of harp music playing in another room.

Cressida wondered if she should look for the unicorns, but as she walked toward a hallway, she heard hooves pounding the ground outside. The noise was so thunderous she wondered if an entire herd of unicorns was stampeding toward the palace. She ran to the window. Looking outside, Cressida saw all seven unicorn princesses racing up the hill toward Spiral Palace, their heads down and their horns pointed straight ahead.

In the lead galloped silver Princess Flash. Behind her sprinted purple Princess Prism. Next trotted blue Princess Breeze, orange Princess Firefly, and black Princess Moon.

Behind all the other unicorns, breathing hard as they trudged uphill, were yellow Princess Sunbeam and green Princess Bloom.

Flash, Prism, Breeze, Firefly, and Moon clattered in through the palace's front door and headed straight for a silver trough of water. They drank quickly and rushed over to Cressida.

"Cressida!" they exclaimed, rearing up on their hind legs. "We were hoping you would come!" Just then, Sunbeam and Bloom dragged themselves into the palace, pink-cheeked and panting. They both nearly fell into the trough, where they guzzled water as though they hadn't had a drink in weeks.

After several seconds, Sunbeam raised her head and grinned at Cressida. "I'm so glad you're here!" Sunbeam said, water dripping from her chin as she tried to catch her breath. "I've missed you so much!" She lowered her head back into the trough for several more gulps before she danced over to Cressida and kneeled down. "Climb up!" she cried. "I'm exhausted from our run, but not too tired to dance around the palace with you on my back!"

Cressida swung her leg over Sunbeam's back, grabbed Sunbeam's silky yellow mane in her hands, and laughed as the unicorn pranced across the room, singing, "My human girl is back! My human girl is back!"

Sunbeam inhaled loudly. "You know, you still don't smell!"

Cressida giggled. Last time she had visited, Sunbeam confessed she had always believed human girls smelled bad. "You don't smell bad, either," Cressida replied.

"That's good, since I've been running all morning," Sunbeam said. Then she blushed and looked down at her hooves. "Well, honestly, I also did a lot of walking. And I took some breaks to sit down and rest. But even still, I'm really, really tired. I hate to say it, but I'm so tired that I think you'd better get off my back."

"No problem," Cressida said, and she slid off Sunbeam.

Flash, who had been stretching on the

other side of the room, joined Cressida and Sunbeam. "You did a great job this morning," Flash said to Sunbeam. "The only way to get better at running is to keep doing it, even when it's hard. That's what I did."

Sunbeam rolled her eyes. "Flash thinks she's better than the rest of us because she goes for a long run every morning," she whispered to Cressida.

"I heard that!" Flash said, but her face broke into a smile. "And I don't think I'm better than all my sisters. I just love to run."

Cressida nodded. She loved to run, too.

"Anyway," Flash said, the magic diamond on her necklace glittering in the light of the chandelier, "I bet you're wondering why we invited you back to the Rainbow Realm."

"Well," Cressida said, "the question had crossed my mind." She couldn't wait to hear what the unicorn princesses were up to.

"So," Flash and Sunbeam said at the same time. They looked at each other. "Well," they both began again.

"I'll tell her," Sunbeam said, sounding annoyed.

"No, I will," Flash said, her voice firm.

"I'm the one that found her," Sunbeam said. "She was my friend first."

Flash sniffed. "The Thunder Dash takes place in my domain. Last time she visited, you got to spend the whole time with her. Now it's my turn."

"But she likes me more," Sunbeam protested.

"No, she likes me more," Flash insisted, flicking her tail and mane.

"Hold on!" Cressida said. "Please stop arguing!"

Sunbeam and Flash, both scowling, looked away from each other.

"Take a deep breath," Cressida said. The unicorns wrinkled their noses. But then they both inhaled slowly and exhaled. "Listen," Cressida said, "I like both of you the same amount, which is a whole, whole lot. I'm sure I'll be able to spend time with both of you during this visit."

Sunbeam and Flash looked calmer, but Cressida could see in their eyes they both still felt a little angry. "Let's take one more deep breath," Cressida said, "the three of us together. And then you can tell me all about the Thunder Dash."

Cressida, Sunbeam, and Flash all sucked in their breath and then exhaled so loudly and forcefully that Flash accidentally snorted. The three of them burst out giggling, and Cressida was relieved to see the sisters looked like they had forgiven each other.

"You can tell Cressida about the Thunder Dash," Sunbeam said. "You're right that it takes place in your domain."

Flash grinned excitedly and swished her

tail. Her eyes glittered. "The reason we invited you here," she began, "is we're going to hold the Thunder Dash this afternoon. I host it every year in my realm, the Thunder Peaks."

"Thanks so much for the invitation," Cressida said. "What, exactly, is the Thunder Dash?"

"It's a running race," explained Flash. "And this year, it will be different than ever before. In the past, only unicorns have competed, and all the other creatures in the Rainbow Realm cheered us on. But this year, we've opened the race to everyone. We were wondering if you want to be the first human girl to run in the Thunder Dash."

Cressida's heart swelled with excitement. She couldn't think of anything that sounded more fun. "I can't wait," Cressida said. She jumped up and down, so her silver unicorn sneakers blinked.

Just then, a lizard wearing a purple cloak and a tall, pointy hat rushed into the room, running upright on his two back feet. He wore blue sneakers with flapping gold wings that lifted him into the air with each step. "Cressida Jenkins? Is it you? The human girl who believes in unicorns?" he asked in a high, nasal voice. Cressida smiled at the funny green creature. "I'm Ernest the wizard-lizard." He held out a hand for Cressida to shake.

"It's a pleasure to meet you," Cressida said, kneeling and trying not to giggle as his cold scales and claws tickled her palm.

"I have a present for you," said Ernest, grinning proudly. And then he reached into the pocket of his cloak and pulled out a pair of gold running shorts and a gold T-shirt with a picture of two silver wings on the front. "I made these for you out of two bananas. It took me a few tries because I kept making teal dirt and cold warts instead of a T-shirt and gold shorts. Can you believe it? But I finally got it right."

Flash, Sunbeam, and all the other unicorn princesses rolled their eyes and smiled at Ernest as Cressida admired her new running outfit. "Thank you so much," Cressida said. She looked at Flash. "Is there somewhere I could change my clothes?"

"No need for that!" called out Ernest. And then he waved his wand at Cressida and chanted, "Changety Switchety Windily Woo! Goldily Clothety Runnily Roo!" Cressida felt wind swirling around her body, as though she stood at the center of a miniature tornado. When the wind stopped, the gold shorts were inside out and upside down on her chest, and the gold shirt hung from her waist like a skirt.

"Oh dear! Oh dear!" said Ernest. "Hold on a minute! Let me try again!" He waved the wand and repeated the spell. Cressida felt another swirl of wind. Then she smiled

with relief. This time the shirt was on top, and the shorts were right side out.

"Thank you, Ernest," Cressida said. "I can't wait to wear my new shorts and T-shirt for the Thunder Dash!"

"No problem!" Ernest said, beaming proudly. Then he looked at Flash. "Um," he said, fidgeting and looking down at his sneakers. "When I was making my new running shoes, there was a bit of a very, very small mishap when I, *ahem*, read the wrong spell. Twice. I'm sure it's nothing. Nothing at all. But, *um*, if you notice anything a little strange in the Thunder Peaks, that's why."

Flash opened her mouth to respond, but before she could say anything, Ernest pulled a watch on a long gold chain from his pocket and cried, "Oh dear! Look at the time! I'd better go! I need to get in one last training run before the Thunder Dash this afternoon." And then he sprinted from the room.

"That Ernest," Flash said, shaking her

head. "He's always up to something. I'm sure I'll find flying lemons or jumping mangos waiting for me when I get back to the Thunder Peaks."

The other unicorn princesses laughed and nodded.

Cressida smiled at the thought of Ernest's magical mishaps. And she was glad she had finally gotten to meet the wizard-lizard she had heard so much about. "It sure was nice of Ernest to make me these new running clothes," she said, twirling around. "How do I look?"

"Fast!" said Flash. "Like a bolt of lightning! You'll be a streak of gold when you run this afternoon."

Sunbeam smiled and nodded, but

Cressida could see in Sunbeam's eyes that the unicorn felt worried and anxious.

Flash noticed, too. "What's wrong?" she asked her youngest sister.

Sunbeam shrugged. "I just don't really want to run in the Thunder Dash this year. I'm sick of always coming in last. It's embarrassing."

"Oh Sunbeam," Flash said. "I've told you a hundred times. If you practiced running more, you'd be faster, and then you'd enjoy the Thunder Dash."

Sunbeam snorted. "You've definitely told me that more than a hundred times. Besides, the only reason you always win is because you cheat. You use your magic to run faster than everyone else."

Hurt and surprise filled Flash's eyes. "I would never cheat. I'm fast because I run every morning, every day of the year. Whenever I invite you to join me, you stop to sunbathe and eat roinkleberries."

"I do not," snapped Sunbeam. "You're a cheater."

"I most certainly am not," Flash said, stomping her hoof.

The other unicorns stared at Flash and Sunbeam. "There they go again," whispered Prism to Breeze. Moon and Firefly nodded. Bloom, who seemed to side with Sunbeam, swished her tail and glared at Flash.

"Please stop shouting," Cressida said. "We all lose our tempers sometimes.

Especially when we feel hurt." She smiled sympathetically at Sunbeam. "It sounds like Flash is proud of how hard she's worked to be a fast runner, and she feels hurt when you accuse her of cheating." And then Cressida looked at Flash. "It sounds like Sunbeam might not like running as much as you do. And that's okay. We can't all be good at everything."

Flash took a long deep breath. Sunbeam sighed. And then they both nodded.

"I'm sorry, Flash," Sunbeam said. She yawned, and her eyelids began to droop. "I'm really tired, and that makes me cranky. I think I'd better take a nap." Cressida noticed Bloom had already fallen fast asleep on a pink velvet couch. Now Sunbeam climbed up next to her sister.

"Apology accepted," said Flash. "Will you and Bloom meet me in the Thunder Peaks after you wake up?"

"Yes," Sunbeam said as her heavy eyelids drooped shut. Soon, both Bloom and Sunbeam were snoring. Cressida smiled at the sight of the yellow and green unicorns curled up together. She hoped Sunbeam would feel better after she slept.

Flash, full of energy, flicked her mane and shuffled her silver hooves. "I'm about to gallop back to the Thunder Peaks to finish preparing for the Dash," she said to Cressida. Want to join me?"

"Of course!" said Cressida.

Flash reared up and whinnied. "I can't wait to show you the Thunder Peaks! Climb up!" she said. "And get ready for a fast ride!"

Chapter Four

Cressida sat on Flash's back and gripped the unicorn's shimmering silver mane. While Sunbeam's mane reminded Cressida of thin threads of yellow silk, Flash's mane seemed more like glittery strands of Christmas tree tinsel. Flash trotted out the palace's front door, and, as soon as her hooves hit the clear stones that led away from Spiral Palace, she began to gallop. As Flash picked up speed, the wind riffled through Cressida's dark hair. Cressida guessed they were going faster than when she glided down a steep hill on her bike or rode a roller coaster at the state fair.

"Want to go even faster?" asked Flash, sounding playful and daring.

Cressida's eyes widened. How could Flash run any faster? "Is that possible?" she called out, laughing.

"As you know, my magic power is to run so fast that my horn and hooves create lightning," Flash explained. "Despite what Sunbeam said, I never use my magic powers when I'm training for the Thunder Dash or in the race itself. But I don't see

any harm in using it now, just for fun. What
do you think?"

"I'm ready!" Cressida said, tightening
her grip on Flash's mane.

And then, suddenly, Flash surged forward, running so fast Cressida wondered if
they were flying. Cressida squealed with
delight as silver and gold lightning bolts
crackled from Flash's horn and hooves.

Now, Cressida was quite sure they were sprinting as fast as a cheetah. "Wheeeeee!" Cressida yelled as Flash sped along a thin, winding forest path. Squirrels and chipmunks stopped chasing each other and searching for nuts to stare at Flash and Cressida. Woodland fairies, with silver wings, called out, "Whoa!" and "Look at them go!" as they peered out from behind giant toadstools. Three baby skunks sprinted alongside Flash and Cressida, trying to keep up, but they soon fell behind and collapsed on the forest floor, breathless and giggling.

Soon, Flash and Cressida came to a long, straight stretch of the forest trail. "Are you ready?" Flash sang out.

Before Cressida could ask, "For what?" Flash leaped into the air, soaring for several seconds before she landed and jumped again.

"We're flying!" Cressida called out as even more lightning sizzled and sparked from Flash's horn and hooves.

Just as Cressida began to feel dizzy and a little sick to her stomach, the trail narrowed and began to turn sharply. Flash slowed down, first to a slow gallop, then a trot, and then a fast walk.

"Phew!" Flash exclaimed, breathless. "That was the most fun I've had in weeks!"

"Me too!" said Cressida.

"I love magic sprinting and leaping even more when you're riding me," said Flash.

"And guess what? We're almost to the Thunder Peaks. So close your eyes!" Cressida shut her eyes and smiled, excited to see Flash's domain. After a few seconds, Flash said, "We're here!"

Cressida opened her eyes to behold a meadow with silvery green, gold, copper, and bronze grass, dotted with blue and purple wildflowers. Copper-colored rabbits, with long ears, hopped through the flowers and chewed on leaves. Golden-orange fox cubs chased each other and tumbled through the grass. Red and bronze butterflies swooped and fluttered. Just behind the meadow towered two of the highest mountains Cressida had ever seen. Minty green pine trees, ferns, and round metallic boulders covered both mountains. In the sunlight, the boulders glittered so brightly Cressida squinted as her eyes adjusted to the light.

"Well? What do you think?" Flash asked, kneeling down so Cressida could slide off her back. Cressida stepped into a patch of silvery green grass, and stared at the meadow and the mountains. They were so stunning Cressida had trouble finding the right words. "Amazing," she finally said. Three baby rabbits jumped over to Cressida and began to nibble the grass. Cressida kneeled down and held out her hand to them. She expected the rabbits to run away, but instead they hopped closer to her. Cressida scooped one up in her

arms, and he nuzzled against her chest and closed his eyes.

Flash glanced at the baby rabbit and smiled. Then she pointed her horn toward one of the Thunder Peaks. "See that path that goes straight up the mountain?" Flash asked. Cressida looked out into the distance as she stroked the baby rabbit's head. She saw a long, bright pink line that started at the base of the mountain and ended at the gold-capped top. "That's the racecourse we use for the Thunder Dash."

"What makes it so pink?" asked Cressida. It was even pinker, Cressida decided, than her favorite pink unicorn raincoat.

"Pink? It's not pi—" Flash began. But her voice trailed off when she lifted her head to look more closely at the mountain. "That's really odd," Flash said slowly. "The path is paved with crushed diamonds. It usually looks white and glittery."

"Should we go check it out?" asked Cressida. Just then, the baby rabbit nudged Cressida's arm and nodded toward the ground. Cressida petted his soft head one more time and placed him back in the patch of grass with his brother and sister.

As Flash and Cressida walked across the meadow toward the pink racecourse, the rabbits nodded at Cressida and the foxes waved. Cressida smiled and waved back. A butterfly landed on her nose, and she giggled until it fluttered away. As

Cressida got closer to the animals, she noticed something funny: many were wearing bright green sneakers.

"Where did all the animals get their running shoes?" Cressida asked.

Flash grinned. "I gave all the creatures in the Thunder Peaks sneakers as a gift. They're very excited to be running in the Thunder Dash for the first time this year."

"I bet," Cressida said.

On the other side of the meadow, at the base of the mountain, Flash and Cressida wove through a thicket of pine trees and then, suddenly, stopped short. "Look at that!" Flash gasped, her eyes wide. There, in front of them, was the start of the path the unicorns used for the Thunder Dash, and it was covered in thick, bright pink mud.

Flash lifted a silver hoof, and touched the pink muck. Immediately, her leg sunk down. "Whoa!" Flash said, laughing. She put another leg into the mud. Then she lifted one of her hooves and stomped down, so pink mud splattered everywhere. Cressida giggled as tiny drops landed on her face, arms, and legs.

"Come on in!" Flash called out, leaping forward so all four hooves sunk into the mud with a giant splash. "I think this is Ernest's best magical mishap yet!"

Cressida giggled and stepped cautiously toward the mud. She wanted to play with Flash, but she also didn't want to ruin her

unicorn sneakers. Just then, her eye caught
something glittery at the base of a pine tree.
She turned and saw two shimmering silver
rain boots with a note on them that read,
**Dear Cressida, It was wonderful to meet
you today. Sincerely, Ernest.** Cressida hur-
riedly took off her sneakers and slipped on
the boots. They fit perfectly.

Flash looked at Cressida's boots and
said, "Those are even shinier than my horn
and hooves!"

Cressida grinned, marched over to the
pink mud, and stepped in. The mud came
halfway up her boots, and it felt thicker and
stickier than she expected.

"Maybe even Sunbeam and Bloom will
like running in this!" Flash said as she

stomped. "We could call this year's race the Thunder-Mud Dash!"

"Or the Thunder *Splash*!" Cressida suggested, twirling and stomping as hard as she could, to splatter the pink mud. Soon, they were both stomping in circles, squealing with delight as pink mud rained down on them.

Then Flash, who had several large globs of pink mud on her nose, paused. She sniffed several times. "Do you smell strawberries?"

Cressida inhaled. Her nose caught only the faintest whiff of strawberries. "I think so," she said slowly.

"I'm sure I do," Flash said. Then, with her silver tongue, she licked the pink mud from her nose. Her eyes widened and she smiled before she lapped up more mud. "Try it!" she said, and she stomped, sending a shower of pink mud right into Cressida's face.

Cressida giggled and wiped off her face with her hand. Then, feeling a little unsure, she licked some of the mud off her fingers. It tasted wonderful and sweet. She laughed. The mud wasn't mud at all. It was strawberry cake batter! And not only that, but it was the best strawberry cake batter she had ever had. "Yum!" Cressida said. She began to lick cake batter off her arms and hands while Flash bowed down and ate some right off the racecourse.

After several minutes of licking the

batter, Flash said, "If I eat any more of this, I'll be too full to run in the Dash!"

"Me too," agreed Cressida.

"Plus," Flash said, "as much fun as we're having, we better get ready for the race. It won't be long before my sisters and all the creatures in the Rainbow Realm arrive ready to run. We need to put up the starting line and the finish line. And we're in a bit of a rush."

"How can I help?" asked Cressida.

"Do you think you could walk up to the top of the mountain and hang the finish line?" Flash asked.

"Definitely!" Cressida said, looking excitedly at the long, pink path leading to the mountain's peak. She couldn't wait to climb up it!

"Great! Thanks, Cressida," Flash said. "I'll stay down here in case anyone gets here early. I'm sure the foxes will be happy to help me hang the starting line and the race flags."

Chapter Five

A fox wearing green sneakers and a yellow visor appeared from behind a boulder carrying a clipboard, two rolled-up ribbons, and a stack of triangular flags.

"Thank you, Frederick," Flash said. "Why don't you give the finish line to my friend, Cressida? She's going to climb up the mountain and hang it for us. And after that, she's going to be the first human girl to run in the Thunder Dash!"

"Well, congratulations!" Frederick said, smiling. "And thanks for your help preparing for the Dash." He handed Cressida one of the ribbons.

"Thank you. I'll be back soon!" she said. She put the finish line in her pocket and began hiking uphill, through the cake batter.

As Cressida walked, the batter got deeper and deeper. Soon, it reached the very tops of her boots. She knew the unicorns would be able to gallop right through it, but she worried the smaller creatures in the Rainbow Realm might struggle to even walk, let alone run, in it. Just then,

Cressida's foot got stuck in an especially thick, deep spot. She tugged and yanked at her boot until it finally came out with a splash.

"Phew!" Cressida said as batter splattered her face.

She decided to take a break from wading through the batter and to instead climb the mountain by scaling the gigantic boulders that covered the Thunder peaks.

She waded over to a gold boulder next to the racecourse, grabbed the top and pulled herself up. As Cressida slid across it, she heard a yawn. And then, for a second, the boulder seemed to jump ever so slightly. Cressida paused, and the boulder stopped moving. She shrugged, leaped to the ground, ran across a log coated in coppery green moss, and began scaling a silver boulder. As soon as she had scrambled to the top, the boulder began to hop.

"Yikes!" said Cressida, almost sliding off.

"Well, hello there!" the boulder called out. "I bet you didn't think you'd be riding a boulder this morning, now did you?"

Cressida laughed. "Hello," she said. After talking to sand dunes and cacti during her last visit to the Rainbow Realm, Cressida wasn't surprised to be conversing with a boulder.

"I'm Boris!" the boulder bellowed, jumping even higher. "Boris the bouncing boulder! And that's Beatrice that you just

climbed over. She's less bouncy than I am today because she went to the Boulder Smolder last night."

"The Boulder Smolder?" Cressida asked. "What's that?"

"Well," said Boris, spinning as he jumped, "we boulders are nocturnal. That means we sleep all day, and we're awake all night."

"Like raccoons and bats," Cressida said. She had learned about nocturnal animals in her science class.

"Precisely!" exclaimed Boris. "Well, every night we boulders hold a Boulder Smolder, where we build a huge bonfire and jump in and out of it! All night long! That makes us good and tired so we can sleep all day."

"Don't you get burned?" Cressida asked.

"Oh no!" laughed Boris. "We boulders love fire. It's never too hot for us. I was planning on going to the Boulder Smolder last night, but I decided to stay home and play with my new marbles. Today I have so much energy I can hardly hold still, let alone sleep."

"I see that," Cressida said, tightening her grip on Boris. She felt as though she were on a trampoline.

"So," Boris said, "who are you, and what brings you to the Thunder Peaks?"

"I'm Cressida Jenkins. I'm friends with Flash."

"Pleasure to meet you!" Boris said.

Just then, Cressida heard two voices calling out from farther up the mountain. "Help!" the voices yelled. "We're stuck! Please help us!"

"Who is that?" Cressida asked, concerned.

"Felicity and Felix," Boris said. "They've

been shouting all morning. I'll take you to them." With that, Boris began to bounce up the mountain.

Every few bounces, he collided with other boulders who yawned and mumbled, "Watch it," and, "I'm trying to sleep."

Finally, Boris landed next to the racecourse, near the mountain's peak. In the middle of the path, poking out of the pink batter, were the heads and tails of two golden-orange foxes.

"My name is Cressida Jenkins," Cressida said, sliding off Boris and rushing over to the edge of the racecourse. "I heard you calling for help."

"Thank goodness!" one of the foxes said. She smiled and her copper eyes twinkled. "My name is Felicity. This is my brother, Felix."

"It's a delight to meet you, even under these strange circumstances," Felix said, twitching his gold whiskers. "We were running this morning when two pink clouds appeared. Then, the next thing we knew, strawberry cake batter rained down on us, and then we got stuck. It was the strangest thing I've ever seen!"

"At least we haven't been hungry while we've been waiting for help," Felicity added as she lapped some batter from her nose.

"I'll certainly try my best to get you out," Cressida said. She reached her arms toward Felicity. "Do you think you can pull out your two front paws and put them in my hands?"

The fox struggled for a few seconds, and then, with a grunt, placed her two front feet in Cressida's palms. Cressida closed her hands tightly around Felicity's green sneakers, both dripping in cake batter.

"One. Two. Three," Cressida counted out loud, and then she pulled as hard as she could. She could feel Felicity straining to lift her hind feet or jump. But the batter was too sticky and thick. Felicity was still stuck.

"Oh no," Felix said, biting his bottom lip. "We'll be here forever."

A tear slid down Felicity's cheek.

"Don't panic yet," Cressida said, trying

to sound reassuring. "I have one more idea." She turned to Boris. "If I lie across you and hold on to Felicity's paws, will you bounce as high as you can?"

"Sure thing!" Boris said.

Cressida climbed onto Boris and again reached out to Felicity. The fox sniffled, took a deep breath, and put her paws back in Cressida's hands.

"Okay, Boris," called out Cressida, "Bounce!"

"That's what I do best!" Boris bellowed as he jumped as high as he could, easily yanking Felicity out of the cake batter.

"Please try to land carefully!" Cressida said, holding tightly to Felicity as the boulder soared toward the sky and then hurtled downward.

To Cressida's surprise, Boris landed gently on a bed of pine needles.

"Phew!" said Felicity, sliding off Boris and twirling around in a circle. "Thank you!" She began to lick cake batter off her arms, legs, stomach, and back.

"I'm glad to help," Cressida said. Then she looked at Boris. "Let's get Felix out."

Cressida climbed onto Boris and grabbed Felix's front feet, which he had managed to yank from the batter. Boris rolled back and launched himself high in the air, pulling Felix with him.

"I'm afraid of heights!" Felix said, sounding panicked as they flew upward.

"I won't let you fall!" Cressida said, squeezing Felix's green sneakers.

Boris landed again in the pine needles. Felix jumped off Boris and ran to hug Felicity. "We're free!" he called out. "Thank you!"

"I'm so glad I could help, and it's been wonderful to meet you," Cressida said. "I hate to hurry off, but I better get up to the top to hang the finish line for Flash. And then I need to tell her we need to get all this cake batter off the racecourse before the Thunder Dash. It's too deep, thick, and sticky for anyone but a unicorn to run through!"

"We'd be glad to hang the finish line while you go talk to Flash," Felicity offered.

Felix nodded. "We know exactly where it goes."

"Thanks!" Cressida said, and she pulled the finish line from her pocket and handed it to Felicity. The two foxes began making their way up the mountain, darting around boulders and climbing logs to get to the top.

"I'll take you to Flash in no time," said Boris, hopping over to Cressida. "Jump aboard!"

Chapter Six

Cressida climbed onto Boris. He bounced down the mountain, crashing into other boulders who yawned and mumbled, "You should have gone to the Boulder Smolder, Boris. You have way too much energy today."

At the bottom of the mountain, Cressida slid off Boris to find Flash at the base of the racecourse giving a team of foxes instructions about where to hang flags and place large troughs of water. "Is the finish line up?" Flash asked.

"Well," said Cressida, "we have a bit of a complication." She told Flash about how thick and deep the cake batter got farther up the racecourse, and about saving Felicity and Felix.

Flash's mouth bent into a worried frown. "Oh no," she said. "The Thunder Dash is supposed to start in less than an hour. How can we possibly clear the course that quickly? I'm worried we'll have to cancel the race." To Cressida's surprise, tears welled up in Flash's eyes.

Cressida put her arms around the

unicorn's silver neck and squeezed. "It's true that we might have to cancel the race," Cressida said. "But before we do, let's see if we can think of a way to quickly clear the course."

Just then, a voice called out from across the meadow: "What's wrong? Did you pull a muscle running?" Cressida and Flash turned to see Sunbeam galloping toward them with Bloom behind her. On Bloom's back rode Ernest, wearing his blue, winged sneakers. Cressida was glad to see that Sunbeam and Bloom now looked much more energetic.

"Look!" said Flash, pointing her horn toward the path. "There's strawberry cake batter all over the racecourse. If we can't think of a way to clean it up, we'll have to cancel the Thunder Dash."

Ernest's bottom jaw dropped. His eyes widened. He slapped both his scaly palms against his forehead. "Oh dear! Oh no!" he called out. "I was thinking there would be just a puddle, or maybe two!"

Flash looked forlornly at the cake batter. "Is there any way to undo the spell?" she asked.

"Well, um, no," said Ernest. "I already looked it up. I'm so sorry, Flash!"

Cressida's heart sank. While she didn't feel as disappointed as Flash, she had been awfully excited to be the first human girl to run in the Dash. "There has to be a way to clean up this cake batter," she said, sucking in her bottom lip exactly the way she did when she was solving a math homework problem.

"I doubt it," said Sunbeam. Cressida turned and saw that Sunbeam did not look even a little disappointed about canceling the Thunder Dash. In fact, Sunbeam's eyes glittered with excitement.

"I can't think of a way to clean it up, either," Bloom added, shrugging. She, too, seemed perfectly happy to skip the race.

"What if we asked all the foxes and rabbits to eat the cake batter?" Cressida suggested.

"That's a good idea, but I think there's just way too much of it," Flash said. "Plus, if they eat cake batter now, they'll feel too sick to run."

Cressida nodded.

"Oh well," said Sunbeam, "I guess we'll just have to cancel the race. Sorry, Flash."

Sunbeam looked like she might start doing a celebratory dance. "Why don't you come join me in my domain, the Glitter Canyon, instead? We can sunbathe in the purple sand. There's even a new patch of violets we can roll around in."

Cressida wasn't in the mood to sunbathe or roll around in violets. She felt like running and racing. "Sunbeam," Cressida said slowly as she stared at the pink batter. "I know your magic power is to control the sun. But you can also make heat come from your horn, right?"

"Sure," said Sunbeam, and she pointed her horn toward the sky. Yellow, sparkling light streamed out, and immediately Cressida felt a gust of hot air.

"And Bloom," Cressida said. "You can make objects grow and shrink, right?"

"Yep," said Bloom, and she pointed her horn toward a copper-colored pinecone on the ground. A beam of emerald light shot from her horn, and the pinecone shrank to the size of a sesame seed. "But I don't know what good that does us now," Bloom said. "Let's go sunbathe!"

"Wait!" exclaimed Cressida, jumping up and down. "I have an idea that will get all the strawberry cake batter off the race-course just in time for the Thunder Dash!"

Flash's eyes widened and sparkled. "What can I do to help?" she asked.

"Well," said Cressida, smiling encouragingly at Sunbeam and Bloom, "we'll mostly need to get help from Sunbeam, Bloom, and the boulders."

Sunbeam's face fell. "I think we should just go sunbathe," she said. "I don't really feel like using my magic right now. I'm still tired from my training run." Bloom nodded in agreement.

"Sunbeam," Cressida said gently, "can we talk for a minute over there?" Cressida pointed to a patch of blue wildflowers under a gnarled copper-and-green pine tree.

"Sure," Sunbeam said. Cressida and Sunbeam walked over to the wildflowers.

"Sunbeam," Cressida said, "it seems like you really don't want to run in the Thunder Dash."

"I'm just really sick of losing. And," she said, letting out a heavy sigh, "yesterday while I was on a training run, the boulders said I look funny when I trot. I used to like running in the Dash. It was fun to run with my sisters, even though I always came in last. But now, after hearing the boulders say that, I don't ever want to run again."

"I can completely understand that," said Cressida. "My older brother used to tease me about how I kicked the soccer ball. I wanted to quit the team, but my parents wouldn't let me. I kept playing, and now soccer is one of my favorite sports. I'm not the best player, but I really enjoy it."

Sunbeam looked thoughtful. "I guess you have a point," she finally said. "If the boulders hadn't said that, I'd still like running in the Dash. I know I shouldn't let them keep me from having a good time. But every time I think about it, I just want the race to be canceled forever."

"Well," said Cressida, "I think the Thunder Dash really means a lot to Flash. So, how about if we go talk to the boulders who teased you. If you feel better afterward, will you help remove the cake batter from the course so Flash doesn't have to cancel the race?"

"Talk to the boulders?" Sunbeam said, looking nervous.

"I'll come with you. And we could even ask Flash to come, too."

Sunbeam took a long, deep breath, as

though she were summoning all her courage. "Okay. I'll try talking to the boulders. And if they apologize and promise not to tease me again, I'll help clear the racecourse. But I don't want Flash to come. I want to prove to myself that I can do this without my big sister's help. Plus, I don't think I can stand to hear her tell me about the importance of practicing even one more time."

Cressida nodded. She often didn't like getting advice from her older brother, either. "Sounds like a good plan," she said. "Which boulders said you looked funny?"

"It was Boris. And his sister Beatrice," Sunbeam said.

"It just so happens I met them this

morning," Cressida said as she and Sunbeam walked together toward the boulders. They found Boris and Beatrice
playing with a set of marbles next to a thick
patch of ferns.

"Boris and Beatrice," said Cressida.
"Sunbeam and I are wondering if we
might talk to you for a moment." The
two boulders looked up. Beatrice looked
sleepy, with droopy gold eyelids, but Boris
seemed wide awake.

"Sure!" bellowed Boris.

"Well—" began Cressida.

But Sunbeam interrupted her. "I
wanted to say," said Sunbeam, "that I felt
really hurt and angry when you said I
looked funny when I was running here

yesterday. I enjoyed running before I heard you say that. And now I feel too self-conscious to race in the Dash."

"Funny?" said Boris, looking confused. He turned to Beatrice. "Did we say Sunbeam looked *funny*?"

"I don't think so," said Beatrice, furrowing her gold brow. "No, not that I can recall. I remember you saying she looked sunny. Like a blur of yellow sunshine."

Recognition came over Boris's face. "That's right! We were watching Sunbeam run, and I called out to her that she looked downright sunny. You know, like a streak of yellow and light." Then he looked back at Sunbeam. "I think you heard us wrong. I never would have said you look funny, because you don't! Plus, that wouldn't be a very nice thing for a boulder, who can't even run, to say about a unicorn. And a unicorn princess at that."

Relief washed over Sunbeam's face. Then she smiled proudly. "Sunny when I run!" she repeated. "Well, thank you for the compliment!"

"You're most welcome," Boris and Beatrice said in unison.

"Sunbeam," Cressida said, "are you willing to help get the racecourse ready for the Thunder Dash?"

"I sure am," said Sunbeam. "Just tell me what you need me to do, and I'll do it!"

"Super," said Cressida. Then she looked at Boris and Beatrice. "I have a plan to get

rid of all that cake batter, but I need the help of all the boulders on the mountain. Do you think you and the other boulders could build an archway over the entire racecourse?"

"An archway?" Boris and Beatrice said at once. "What's that?"

"Well," Cressida said. She knew all about archways because she and Corey liked to build them out of blocks. "It's a passageway shaped like an upside down *U*." She used her hands to show Boris and Beatrice what an archway looked like.

Boris and Beatrice looked at each other and nodded. Boris bellowed, "One archway made of boulders coming right up!" Then, with huge grins, he and Beatrice

began bouncing up the mountain shouting, "Attention all boulders! Wake up! It's
time to build an archway over the racecourse! Get up and build an archway!
I repeat! Get up and build an archway!"

Chapter Seven

As the boulders jumped and hopped toward the racecourse, Cressida and Sunbeam sprinted back to Flash, Bloom, and Ernest.

Cressida looked at Bloom and said, "Sunbeam and the boulders have agreed to help us get this cake batter off the racecourse. Bloom, will you help us, too?"

Bloom looked at Sunbeam and narrowed her eyes. "Are you sure?" she asked Sunbeam.

"I'm sure," said Sunbeam, nodding. "I'll tell you all about it later. I feel much better now. It turns out there was a bit of a misunderstanding."

Bloom shrugged. "If Sunbeam is willing to help, I am too."

Flash opened her mouth—probably to ask Sunbeam and Bloom what they were talking about—but then, thinking better of it, she just smiled, relieved her sisters were going to help save the Thunder Dash.

"Fantastic!" said Cressida. She turned around toward the racecourse, and, to her amazement, she saw that the boulders had already stacked themselves into a perfect archway that stretched the entire length of the path. "That was quick," Cressida said. "Now we have our very own, huge oven." She looked at Sunbeam. "Do you think you could shoot heat from your horn into the archway?"

Sunbeam looked hesitant. "Won't it burn the boulders?"

"The boulders love heat so much they spend every night jumping in and out of bonfires," Cressida explained.

Flash nodded. "I promise you won't hurt them."

"Well, I'll give it a try!" said Sunbeam. She walked over to the racecourse, pointed her horn toward the inside of the archway, and shot out a golden beam of light and heat.

The boulders immediately cheered. "This is great!" Boris yelled. "It's even better than bouncing in a bonfire."

Soon enough, the batter darkened to a deeper shade of pink and began to rise. When it turned golden at the top, Cressida said, "Okay, Sunbeam! I think that's enough."

Sunbeam stopped the beam of yellow light coming from her horn. "I've never baked a cake before," she said, smiling.

Next, Cressida called out, "Thank you, boulders, for your help! That was an amazing archway! Now you can go back to your spots on the mountain."

Immediately, Boris and Beatrice began to bounce and shout, "Everyone up! Time to go home! Up up up!"

The boulders unstacked themselves, exclaiming, "That was more fun than a Boulder Smolder!" and, "We should do that again!"

Now, instead of a coating of thick, sticky, strawberry cake batter on the racecourse, there was a huge pink cake. It was the longest, thickest cake Cressida had ever seen. "Are we going to run on that?" Flash asked, sounding a little nervous. "I guess we could call the race the Cake Dash. But that name isn't very catchy."

"Nope!" said Cressida. "Bloom, do you

think you could shrink this cake, so it's small enough to move off the racecourse, but big enough for all of us to eat after the race?"

"Sure thing!" said Bloom, and she pointed her shiny green horn right at the huge pink cake. She shot out a glittery green beam of light, and almost instantly the cake began to shrink, until it was the size of a large bed.

"Could you please help me move this beautiful, strawberry cake off the race-course?" Cressida asked Ernest. The wizard-lizard rushed over, and the two of them picked up the cake and gently set it down next to the starting line.

"How about if I whip up some frosting?" said Ernest excitedly. "I think I remember the spell. It's—"

But before he could finish, Flash, Bloom, and Sunbeam all shouted, "No! No more spells!" Then they all laughed, even Ernest.

Flash leaped onto the racecourse, which was paved in glittering crushed diamonds and an occasional pink cake crumb. "Oh Cressida!" Flash called out. "Thank you! You saved the Thunder Dash!"

Chapter Eight

As all the creatures in the Rainbow Realm lined up to run in the Thunder Dash, Cressida thought that she had never seen such a colorful crowd. Up in front were the princess unicorns—Flash, Sunbeam, Bloom, Moon, Breeze, Prism, and Firefly—stretching their legs and striking their hooves against the ground. Behind them, running in place and touching their toes, were throngs of foxes, rabbits, mountain goats, squirrels, cats, skunks, lizards, frogs, and turtles, all in vibrant colors—teal, green, red, purple, pink, magenta, neon orange, blue, and black. At the back were strangely colored spiders, ants, bees, slugs, snails, butterflies, and grasshoppers. Cressida even spotted several fairies beating their filmy wings, and a small herd of miniature dragons puffing fire as they stretched their legs.

Cressida found her silver unicorn sneakers next to a pine tree near the base of the racecourse. She pulled off her glittery boots, wishing she could take them home with her, and put on her running shoes. Then she took her place behind the starting line next to the unicorns, even though she knew as soon as the race started, they would run far ahead of her.

Flash climbed onto Beatrice, who sat next to the starting line smiling sleepily. "Attention!" Flash called out. "Attention!"

The crowd quieted.

"It's my honor to welcome all of you to the annual Thunder Dash!"

The crowd cheered.

"This is a very special year," Flash continued. "For the first time, we've opened up the race to all the creatures in the Rainbow Realm. And that includes our very first human girl runner, Cressida Jenkins." The crowd clapped and cheered even more loudly, and Cressida's heart fluttered in her chest. Flash winked at Cressida before she yelled, "When Beatrice bellows, the race will begin!" The crowd quieted. Flash climbed off the boulder and took her place behind the starting line.

"Go!" Beatrice bellowed, so loudly Cressida jumped in surprise.

Immediately, the princess unicorns bolted forward, their metallic hooves a blur against the crushed diamond path. Flash pulled into the lead. Behind her were Prism, Breeze, Moon, and Firefly. And behind them were Bloom and Sunbeam. All around Cressida were jogging creatures. Ernest sprinted by her, his purple hat bobbing as his blue, gold-winged sneakers carried him forward. Foxes in green

sneakers, including Felicity and Felix, passed Cressida. A rainbow-colored cat trotted by, proudly twitching her tail. Cressida, in her silver sneakers, was glad that she was at least faster than the turtles, the spiders, the ants, and the grasshoppers.

The boulders, lined up along the race-course, cheered on the runners.

Just when Cressida was starting to lose her breath, and her legs were starting to get tired, she saw the finish line ahead. With her heart thundering in her chest, she pushed herself to run as fast as she could. With every last bit of energy, she sprinted to the finish line, leaping across as her sneakers blinked.

At the top of the mountain, Cressida

gulped down two cups of water and found the unicorns standing by a silver trough. Flash, as always, had won the race, and she wore a gold medal. Prism, who had come in second, wore a silver medal. Breeze, wearing a bronze medal, had finished third.

"Congratulations!" Cressida said, looking at Flash, Prism, and Breeze. Then she looked at Sunbeam.

"Guess what?" Sunbeam said to Cressida. "I ran the fastest I've ever run before. I had my best time yet. I think it was because I could hear Boris and Beatrice cheering me on. They told me I looked sunny!"

"Wow! That's great!" Cressida said.

"I'm very proud of my littlest sister," Flash said. "This really is my favorite day of the year. Thank you, Cressida, for being the very first human girl to run in the

Thunder Dash. It's been our honor to have you."

"It's been my honor to run," said Cressida, grabbing another cup of water. She didn't think she had ever run so fast or so hard in her life.

"I know you'll need to go home soon," Flash said, and Cressida nodded. She had to admit she was tired and ready to see her parents and Corey. "But before you go, please have a piece of cake. Boris bounced it all the way up to the finish line so we could enjoy it."

Ernest, still wearing his blue winged shoes, jogged over to Cressida. He held two forks and two plates of strawberry cake, each piled high with the brightest yellow frosting Cressida had ever seen. "I couldn't help myself. A cake needs frosting!" Ernest said, blushing.

"Thank you," said Cressida, and she began to cut off a small bite of cake with her fork.

Ernest shoveled a huge mound of pink cake and yellow frosting into his scaly mouth, and then his face fell. "Oh dear! You better not eat that."

"Why not?" Cressida asked, putting down her fork.

Ernest smiled sheepishly. "Well, I meant to make cranberry-flavored frosting, but it seems I made canary-flavored frosting by accident. I feel like I have a mouth full of feathers. Don't worry. There were no real canaries involved."

Cressida began to giggle. "Oh Ernest," she said. "Don't worry about it."

Just then, Cressida's stomach rumbled. But what she really wanted to eat, instead of cake, was a peanut butter and banana sandwich, some carrot sticks with hummus, blueberry yogurt, and maybe, if she was still hungry after all that, an apple.

Flash caught Cressida's eye and walked over. "You look like you might be about ready to go back to the human world," she said.

"Well," Cressida said. "It's true I'd like to eat some human food. And I miss my parents and Corey."

Flash nodded. "It was a pleasure to have you as our guest in the Rainbow Realm. Thank you so much for saving the Thunder Dash."

"I had such a great time today," said Cressida. "Thank you so much for inviting me!"

Flash, Sunbeam, Bloom, Prism, Firefly, Moon, and Breeze surrounded Cressida. "Thank you so much for coming!" they called out. "Come back soon!"

"And remember," Sunbeam said, "you're welcome back anytime. And when we want to signal for you to visit us for a special reason, we'll make your key turn bright pink. Do you promise you won't forget?"

Cressida laughed at the idea that she

could ever forget. "I promise," said Cressida. With that, Cressida pulled her key from her pocket and put both hands on the crystal handle. "Take me home, please!" Cressida said. The Thunder Peaks began to spin and spin into a quickening blur of silver, gold, copper, and bronze. Cressida felt as though she were soaring through the air, higher and higher. And then, with a gentle *thud*, she found herself sitting at the base of the oak tree in the woods behind her house. Cressida stood up slowly and smiled. She was wearing her rainbow leggings and her blue unicorn sweater again. But she felt something heavy and unfamiliar around her neck. She looked down, and there hung a gold medal with pink sequins.

On the front was a picture of a running uni-corn. And on the back, in engraved letters,

it said, CRESSIDA JENKINS, FIRST HUMAN GIRL TO RUN IN THE THUNDER DASH.

Cressida smiled. And then, though her legs were tired, Cressida ran home, her sneakers blinking and her medal swinging across her chest.

DON'T MISS OUR NEXT MAGICAL ADVENTURE!

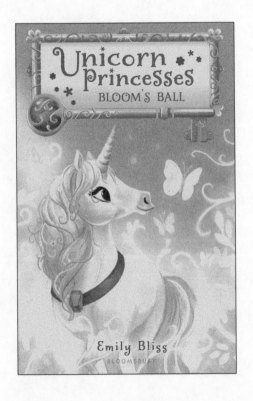

TURN THE PAGE FOR A SNEAK PEEK . . .

In the top tower of Spiral Palace, Ernest, a wizard-lizard wearing a pointy purple hat and a matching cape, put three apricots on a chair. Above him, two tomatoes, each with bright yellow wings, swooped down from a bookshelf. Near the window, three silver-winged bananas hovered. A flock of plums fluttered their gold wings around a chandelier.

Ernest cleared his throat and raised his wand. But as he opened his mouth to begin casting a spell, he heard a knock on the door. "Come in!" he called out.

The door opened, and in stepped Princess Bloom, a green unicorn with a magic emerald that hung around her neck on a purple ribbon. In her mouth, she carried a blue velvet bag. Bloom smiled as she admired Ernest's flying tomatoes, bananas, and plums. Then she dropped the bag between her shiny green hooves and said, "You sure have been working hard on your flying spells. It looks like you've finally gotten the hang of it."

Ernest blushed. "I've been practicing for weeks," he said. "At the beginning, all the fruits and vegetables grew springs instead of wings. There were oranges and peaches bouncing and boinging all over the room. But now they sprout wings, usually on my first or second try."

Just then, a swooping tomato collided with a plum right above Ernest's head. With a *splat*, the tomato landed on the pointed tip of Ernest's hat. "Not again," he groaned as red juice dripped into his eyes.

Bloom giggled.

"Anyway," Ernest said, wiping his face with his cape, "what brings you to my tower?"

"I was wondering," Bloom said, "if you might use your magic to help me."

Ernest grinned with delight. The unicorn

princesses mostly teased him about his spells, which often seemed to go wrong. It was unusual for a creature in the Rainbow Realm to ask for his magical assistance. "I'd be most honored," he said, dabbing a final drop of tomato juice from his long, green nose.

Bloom opened the velvet bag and pulled out a stack of lime-colored, glittery envelopes. "These are invitations to my birthday party this afternoon," she explained. "I'm about to take them to the mail-snails to deliver. But there's one invitation I wanted to send in a special way." Bloom passed an especially glittery envelope to Ernest. On the front, it said,

To My Sister and Best Friend,

Princess Prism

"As you know," Bloom continued, "Prism likes anything that's playful and creative. And she loves surprises. I was wondering if you could cast a spell on the invitation so it grows wings and flies to her."

"Absolutely!" Ernest exclaimed, jumping up and down. "And I know exactly which spell to use. It's in my favorite book, *Wings on Things*, volume three. Or is it volume two?" Ernest scratched his forehead.

A look of concern crossed Bloom's face. "Are you absolutely sure you can do it?"

"Oh yes!" Ernest said. "I promise I won't make any mistakes."

"In that case," said Bloom, "thank you so much for your help. And now I'd better hurry to take the rest of the invitations to the mail-snails. If I don't drop them off now, the mail-snails won't have enough time to deliver them before the party starts." She smiled sheepishly. "You know me! I have trouble doing almost anything before the last minute." With that, Bloom pushed the rest of the envelopes back into the velvet bag, grabbed the sack in her mouth, and rushed out the door.

As soon as Bloom was gone, Ernest raced over to a bookshelf and pulled down a thick, black book. He flipped through the pages and stopped on page 147.

Rubbing his scaly hands together, he exclaimed, "Bloom and Prism will love this!"

He put Prism's invitation on the table. He picked up his wand. And he chanted, "Happety Bappety Birthday Bloom! Wingety Swingety Fluttery Sloom! Glittery Flittery Slittery Sail! Prettily Flittery Slittery Quail!"

Ernest waited. Nothing happened. The envelope didn't even jump or tremble, and there certainly weren't any wings—or even springs—growing from it.

"Oh dear!" Ernest said, hitting his forehead with his palm. "Did I say 'quail' instead of 'mail'? Oh dear!"

Just then, thunder rumbled, and Ernest sprinted to the window in time to see several bolts of purple light flashing in the distance.

"Not again," Ernest groaned. "Hopefully, nothing will go wrong until after Bloom's party."

He shrugged and returned to the envelope. He checked the book again. And then he waved his wand and chanted, "Happety Bappety Birthday Bloom! Wingety Swingety Fluttery Sloom! Glittery Flittery Slittery Sail! Prettily Flittery Slittery Mail!" This time, the invitation spun around and two tiny, sparkling green wings sprouted from one of its corners. "Oh dear," Ernest said. "Those wings are awfully small."

The envelope flapped its wings and rose a few inches into the air. "Well, at least it can fly," Ernest said, shrugging. He carried the envelope to the open window. "Off you go to Princess Prism," he said. The envelope jumped off his hand and began to flutter, ever so slowly, down the side of Spiral Palace.

Emily Bliss lives just down the street from a forest. From her living room window, she can see a big oak tree with a magic keyhole. Like Cressida Jenkins, she knows that unicorns are real.

Sydney Hanson was raised in Minnesota alongside numerous pets and brothers. She has worked for several animation shops, including Nickelodeon and Disney Interactive. In her spare time she enjoys traveling and spending time outside with her adopted brother, a Labrador retriever named Cash. She lives in Los Angeles.

www.sydwiki.tumblr.com